Story B

and The Snowbird Ballet

By **Yolanda King**
Pictures By **Pia Reyes**

Story Bird Dance

and The Snowbird Ballet

Summary: The first winter recital for Story Bird Dance Academy is around the corner and the dancers are nervous about their parts. Jada is afraid to dance in front of the big kids and Nia's costume really looks like it has scales, which she absolutely dislikes. The show must go on. Will Sky be able to help her two best-friends face their fears?

ISBN 978-0-9910272-8-6

TANGLED
PRESS

www.TangledPress.com

For Riley, Naome, Azana, Zarina, Zahira & Zinnia

Don't miss the first Story Bird Dance book

Story Bird Dance
and the Haunted Studio

Table of Contents

Chapter One
Letters

"I don't want to open it," Nia said, sliding from the fluffy purple beanbag onto the purple flower-shaped rug. Her hands rested behind her touching the wood floor. "What if I'm the Lizard

King? Open yours first," she said, nodding at Sky.

"Really Nia? You're going to let a little fear of reptiles keep you from dancing one of the best parts in the winter recital?" said Sky.

"Uh, yes," said Nia. "I like birds, rabbits, bears and dogs and cats and hamsters. I don't do scales."

Sky took a deep breath and shook her head. "Let's just wait for Jada and we'll open the letters together."

Ms. Kenya, the girls' dance teacher and owner of Story Bird Dance Academy, had mailed each student a letter announcing their parts in the winter recital. This was the school's first year performing during the winter. Ms. Kenya said she felt inspired by the coming cold days and decided to write and choreograph the modern ballet story The Snowbird for her students.

"Hey guys, so sorry I'm late," Jada said, rushing into the room. "My mom took forever finishing these two French braids. You'd think a psychologist would know better than trying to get the perfect center part." She dropped her coat onto the bed and pulled off

her hat. "What'd I miss?"

Nia patted a space next to her on the rug. She and Sky were sitting with their legs crossed. They both scooted to the edge of the rug and closer to the purple polka dot-covered bed.

"Well one, Nia is still afraid of crawly things with scales," said Sky. "Two, why are you wearing a wool hat when your mom just did your hair?"

"It's freezing outside and I don't want to catch a cold," said Jada. "I could miss school if I get sick. It's well documented that you have to protect your head and feet in the winter.

And Nia, I don't blame you. Sky, you remember those costume sketches Ms. Kenya showed us of the Lizard King costume? The glittery red, black and brown scales are lovely, but the crooked red hanging skin make me say ewww."

"That's what I was thinking, but I could totally rock the Snowbird, Arctic Hare or Polar Bear outfit. Feathers or fur look pretty good on me," said Nia. "But I think we can all cross out getting the Polar Bear parts. Zane or Ben will probably get them. Ms. Kenya has the bears lifting the hares during some of the leaps."

Sky sighed at both of her friends. "Ok ladies, let's get down to business. Jada did you bring your letter?"

"Sure did," said Jada waving her letter and sitting on the floor of Nia's room.

"Ok, on the count of three, everyone open your letter. One, two, three, open." The girls each broke the seal of their blue envelops and scanned the letters from Ms. Kenya.

Sky checked the faces of each of her closest friends, looking and hoping for the excitement she was feeling.

Ms. Kenya wrote several different characters into her ballet story. The Lizard King and Snowbird were the two leading *antagonist* and *protagonist* characters. The Polar Bears and Arctic Hares had a major dance battle scene with the Lizard King and his minions, the Leaf Lizards.

She was just about to ask her friends what their parts were when Nia's mom poked her head in the door and asked, "Anyone want to try some hot chai tea and ginger peppermint cookies? I know today is a big day." The girls loved going to Nia's house. Her mom had a pastry *catering* busi-

ness and was constantly experiment-
ing with different cookie recipes. This
winter she was adding teas to her business.

"Thank you, Mrs. Starr," the girls
called out in unison. Mrs. Starr set a

tray in front of the girls and kissed the top of Nia's head and gave the other girls a quick head massage. "I wasn't always a mom and cookie expert. My college dance professor always reminded us that the most important thing is that you get better each time you practice."

"Yes ma'am," the girls said, as Nia's mom left the purple bedroom.

"Ok guys, who wants to go first?" said Sky.

Chapter Two
Meltdown

The house was so quiet, you could hear the crackling fire in the living room and the cold wind blowing outside. The friends silently read their letters, but their faces and bodies spoke loud and clear.

Nia sat with her head tilted and eyes squinting behind her cat-styled glasses. She was taking deep breaths.

Jada dropped her letter and frowned up to the ceiling, hugging her body. "I'm an Arctic Hare," she erupted with no warning. "I have to mirror the exact movements of four other dancers for two different songs... two very long songs. You know I have a hard time keeping up with them? Oh man, what if I forget my steps or the Polar Bear drops me? Could that even happen?"

Jada stood up and started walking around the tiny room. "If I mess up, everyone will see I'm not doing the right steps. My parents will be in the audience and they'll want to invite their friends and my grandparents. Wait a minute, the big dancers will be in the audience too. In the front row. Watching my every move! What was I thinking being excited about this recital!?"

"Jada, relax," Nia said, gently touching one of her friend's pacing feet.

"Yes, Jada, let's take a rest and

some deep breaths," said Sky.

Jada sat on her bottom and leaned against Nia's bean bag.

"Remember when Ms. Kenya did a run through of the parts? The Arctic Hare dances were the ones you cheered for the loudest. Especially when the hare dances with the Forget Me Not Fairies. You love working with the little dancers. They're counting on you. Plus, you said the music told the entire story. So, let the music *cue* you," said Sky.

"And the big kids look out for us, like we look out for the little dancers," said Nia. "Besides Ms. Kenya would be so mad if they weren't encouraging. I'm talking blowout, EPIC FAIL."

Ms. Kenya expected her students to work hard both in the dance studio and at everything they tried. She gave her dancers critiques and celebrated their successes and did not tolerate others behaving in a way that would cause someone pain or doubts about themselves. She was all about the process of becoming a stronger person and better dancer.

"Zane and Ben have been working out. I've seen them doing pushups and lots of running at soccer prac-tice. They'll be able to support you, I promise," said Sky.

Chapter Three
Lizards

"Well now that we've got that settled...my worst nightmare is real," Nia said. "I'm the Lizard King!" Nia went from sitting up, to laying down with her knees bent, heels touching.

She seemed to be looking for answers in the quiet ceiling fan.

"Nia, it's not so bad," said Sky. "The Lizard King is like a really cool villain and you'll get to do tons of leaps. That's like a dream come true for you."

"Plus there's only one Lizard King and no one will know if you mess up," Jada said, still thinking about her hare group dance.

"I'm not worried about messing up. It's just that snakes, lizards, even turtles freak me out. I don't do reptiles," groaned Nia.

"What don't you like about them?"

asked Sky.

"Well they stick out their tongues at the most random times," said Nia.

"That's how some of them pick smells out of the air Nia. Plus, that's not true for all reptiles," Jada said.

"There's more," said Nia. "They don't have belly buttons!"

"Talk about random," said Sky. "Nia, are you serious? Those are your reasons for not wanting to be the Lizard King in the ballet?" asked Sky.

"No. There's way more. Plastic toy snakes and lizards look so real. My cousin left one under the kitchen table.

I dropped a hot pan of my mom's kale banana brownies when I saw it just laying there on the floor.

There should be a rule, not to make them so real-looking. Like they do with toy weapons. They could stamp a big orange smiley face on the back of all reptile toys. Plus, their eyes...they just stare at you. Like they're daring you to move. I don't think they ever blink. It creeps me out."

"Ok, I'm with her on that one," said Jada. "I once had a staring contest with my brother's pet gecko, Mr. Greedo. I'm pretty sure it was trying to hypnotize me."

"Jada, you're the best. That is not a part of my fear, but thanks for *empathizing* with me," said Nia, patting her friends shoulder.

"Fine," shrugged Jada. "But do we really know what the reptilian nation is thinking? You won't catch me staring deeply into Mr. Greedo's eyes ever again."

"Cheese and crackers. Are you guys kidding me?" asked Sky. Sometimes Sky said the oddest things to get her friends attention. She'd been doing this since they were in the three-year-old dance class and pretending to have their own dance studio like Ms. Kenya. Over the years the girls keep combining their interest and including more business ideas. "How are we going to open our Veterinary-Dance-Sports clinic when we're older?"

"No worries, I've got it all figured out," said Nia. "Plan A, we won't service reptiles. Plan B, we have reptile days. You guys can run the vet clinic on those days and I'll handle the dance and sports classes. When the mammals or belly button-owning animals come for a visit, we switch. I'll run the clinic while you two run the studios. BAM, problem solved."

Jada sat considering the possibilities. "Plan B could work. Although I may want to skip some reptile days too."

Sky smiled patiently. She was used to her friends getting off track. "Nia and Jada, we can totally rock this recital. My mom and Ms. Kenya say we can do anything we put our minds and bodies towards. This will be Story Bird Dance Academy's first winter recital. And, according to my letter, you guys are looking at the winter recital Snowbird; and Snowbirds lay diamond eggs that can see the future."

"Ohhhh, congratulations on being the Snowbird, Sky!" said both friends, rushing to hug tackle their bestie. "You worked so hard all year."

Nia's mom Mrs. Starr stuck her head back into the room. "Sky and Jada, your parents are here to pick you up. Who wants to tell me about the recital as you grab some to-go cookies?"

Chapter Four
Fitting

The girls stepped across the newly repaired front porch of the dance studio. You could still smell the freshly cut cedar. A view through the large glass pane in the oak door showed the rooms branching out left and right from the foyer and a staircase in the middle leading to more classes. Sky took off one glove to turn the cold doorknob. A chime rang as the door opened. They placed their shoes in the foyer cubbies and climbed the stairs for a meeting about the recital.

Zane met the girls at the top of the stairs. "You'll never guess what part I have in the recital? Sky, don't say anything," said Zane glancing at his little sister.

"Hmmm, let me think. The mortally wounded Polar Bear at the end?"

said Nia.

"Hey, why didn't you guess the Lizard King? I could be the Lizard King," said Zane, walking the girls to the front of the mirror-lined studio.

"Because, I'm the Lizard King and would gladly switch with you," Nia said.

"Do not ask Ms. Kenya to switch your parts. I don't want Nia lifting me when I leap," said Jada.

"No problem there. I got a peek at the costumes Ms. Kenya was ordering and there's no way I'm wearing that shiny Lizard King leotard," said Zane.

"See, even Zane thinks lizards are gross," said Nia.

"I didn't say that," said Zane. "I just don't want to wear that costume. Lizards are cool. I'm trying to convince our mom to get me a bearded dragon."

Ms. Kenya and Tuesday's dance assistant, Araiya, walked in pushing an overflowing wardrobe rack. Labeled black bags hung from the top rack. "Lovelies, great news. Our costumes arrived a few days early," said Ms. Kenya, clapping her elegant fingers.

The students thought everything

about Ms. Kenya was *sophisticated*.

From the tip of her coily black ponytail

to her turned out toes. Ms. Kenya often stood in *first position*, just because.

"Who wants to try on costumes today?" she asked. Twelve pairs of arms flew into the air.

"Me! I do" they yelled.

Ms. Kenya held up a hand and the students became silent. "Hear me out please. Try on your costume. Let me or Araiya see you. Then return it to your garment bag for safe keeping. When your parents get here, take it home until the recital. Okay, let's get started...."

"What do you think?" asked Sky

as she helped adjust Jada's fuzzy tan and white leotard.

"Let's see how it looks when I put on these floppy ears. They're so fluffy" said Jada.

"Don't forget your tail and shoes," said Nia. "Those shoes will make great hare tracks through the production snow."

"How in the world did the seamstress get my ballet shoes to look so soft?" asked Jada. "I could rub them all day."

"I don't know, but a better question is how did she get these scales to look so real on my leotard," said Nia, shuddering. "Maybe I'll dance with my eyes closed."

"Nia, you look fantastic!" Sky and Jada said at the same time. They turned to each other and said, "Jinx you owe me a soda!" and fell out laughing.

"That's easy for you to say. You're both wearing beautiful scale-free costumes. Sky, the Snowbird looks chic and I love how your headpiece sits like a crown on your head."

"You're all looking marvelous," Ms. Kenya said as she came by to check their outfits. "Let's see how these costumes move. Everyone to the end of the room and we'll *chasse-tour-jete* across the floor in pairs. Get tall. Get ready. Five, six, seven, eight....

Chapter Five

Plans

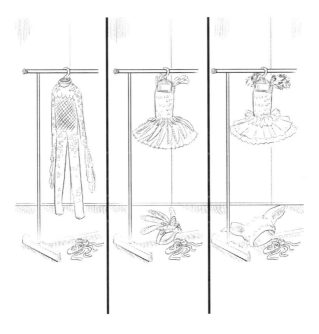

"Class was fun," said Sky, taking a drink from her water bottle. A few bundled students were sitting on the porch waiting for their parents' to pick them up, other stood watch from inside the toasty studio. A chilly wind blew through the trees and a few brown leaves leisurely floated from the branches.

"Do you think it'll snow this year?" asked Jada. "Maybe there'll be a huge blizzard and everyone will have to stay home, including the big kids, and the Snowbird recital will have to be postponed."

"Jada, you're dreaming out loud," said Nia. "It snows about every four or five years in Story Bird, Texas and even then it's like two inches."

"A girl can dream," said Jada.

"I know what you mean. I'm

trying so hard not to touch this lizard leotard. I'm hoping it'll magically turn into cotton candy," said Nia.

"Hey, you guys better not mess up this recital. I invited my entire soccer team and coaches to see me play a Polar Bear," said Zane finishing his second almond butter and jelly sandwich of the day.

"I've got an idea," said Sky, standing up to punch her brother on the shoulder.

"Please share, but share quickly. It's getting cold out here," said Nia.

"Ok here's what we need to do.

For Jada, we'll hang out with the big kids. Go to their practices, eat with them, dance with them, find out what they like, then Jada will see that they're normal and not to be feared."

"We don't have that much time," said Nia.

"Ok, better idea, let's just focus on one big kid, Araiya," said Sky. "She's super nice and she's the queen of the big kids. It'll be like submerging therapy."

"What's submerging therapy?" asked Jada.

"You know, submerging," said Sky.

"I heard your mom talk about it, Jada. When you spend a lot of time around something you don't like. Submerging therapy. We have to face our fears."

"Oh you mean immersion therapy," said Jada. "Is that what it's called?"

"Then that's what I mean. Immersion therapy... for both of you," said

Sky.

"Nia, we'll go to Dr. Washington's Fuzzy Friends Veterinary clinic for some real reptile time," said Sky.

"Good idea. I can even bring my brother's pet gecko," said Jada.

Chapter Six

Listen

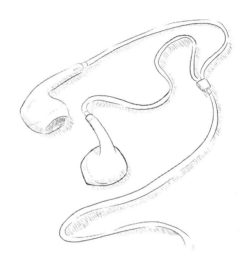

"Remind me why we're an hour early for practice again," Jada said as they stood in the foyer of the dance academy peeling off their winter jackets.

"Come on, the Snowbird can see

into the future and knows all," Sky laughed. "Do you want to get used to dancing in front of the big kids or not?" She reached to turn the knob on the girls' changing room door. All three girls walked in and dropped their bags on the wall near the lockers. There were older students sitting on the wooden benches. Some with faces dedicated to their phones and a few on the floor stretching.

Nia pointed towards a girl resting on the blue couch. She had one long brown leg curled under her and the other was gently tapping the floor. Her eyes were closed and her head swayed to the music coming out of her head-phones. One polished hand waved through the air, conducting an invisible orchestra.

"Maybe we should come back another time," Jada whispered, chomping on one of her braids and turning to leave. "She looks busy to me."

"We have to do it now. Winter recital is next week," said Sky, turning Jada around.

"Come on Jada, you can do this," said Nia.

Sky and Nia gently pushed Jada in front of them and steered her around

the benches and dancers. Sky gave Jada a gentle nudge once they were standing near the couch. "Go ahead say something."

"Umm, Araiya, how's your day going?" Jada asked. Araiya didn't change positions or look up. Jada turned to her friends and quietly mouthed "Now what?"

"Stand closer and keep trying," they whispered.

Jada took a deep breath and glanced at the other big kids around the room. They weren't paying the young dancers any attention. "Araiya, I like your hair bun."

Nia and Sky both pointed their fingers towards their ears. "Jada, she can't hear you with those earbuds on," said Nia. "You've got to get her attention."

Jada sighed and stepped closer to the couch. This time she tapped Araiya on the shoulder. Araiya's hand stopped moving midair and she looked up at Jada. A smile spread across her face when she saw the three young dancers. She plucked the earbuds out of her ears. "Hey girlies, what are you guys doing here? Modern dance doesn't start for an hour."

"We have a problem" said Sky. "Actually, Jada has a problem and we thought you could help."

"I'd love to help. Sit right here Jada. Tell me what's on your mind," Araiya said patting the cushion next to her.

Jada took a deep breath and slow exhale, then shared how she was nervous about what the big kids would think of her dancing. She told Araiya how she wanted all her steps to be perfect and when they weren't, it felt like the whole world was watching.

"I wish I had a time machine and a memory swiper. That way, each time I messed-up, I could press a restart button and no one would realize my mistakes," said Jada.

Araiya listened to the girl's *dilemma*. At times she frowned and nodded her head. When they were done she said, "Oh Jada, we're a family here. We all love watching you guys dance. You are strong dancers and inspire us to do even better. We're all cheering for you. Each time you learn a new step or take the stage you're being brave. Practice and focus are a must. Perfect is not required. I used to be a little dancer and remember feeling self-conscious in front of small crowds. Big crowds didn't bother me, but for some reason small audiences did. Maybe because I could see each person's face and realized they could see me too."

"You know what helps me?" Araiya continued, asking Jada.

"No, tell me," said Jada.

"When I dance, I dance for me. It makes me happy. I imagine all the theatre seats are filled with my pet dog, Diggers. It helps me forget the audience. Diggers loves to watch me.

Sometimes he gets so excited he starts twirling and bumping into me while I dance."

"That's funny," said Jada.

"I know, right?" said Araiya. "He thinks he's dancing too and then forgets and starts chasing his tail."

The girls all grinned and laughed at the image of Diggers turning in circles.

"Is there someone or something you could put in the audience to help you concentrate on your love of dance?" Araiya asked Jada.

Jada thought for a minute. Her

hands were shoved into the pockets of her warmup hoodie. "There's my bunny, Flopsy," she said. "My uncle Troy got her for me when I was born. She sleeps with me, goes on trips with me and sometimes I put her in my backpack and take her to school with me."

"Wow, you take a rabbit to school? Your teachers don't get upset?" asked Araiya. The girls giggled.

"Flopsy is not a real rabbit. It's Jada's stuffed bunny. She's soft and gray and has crazy long ears," said Sky.

"Oh," said Araiya, joining the girls

in the giggle. "Flopsy would be the perfect audience filler for you Jada."

"Thanks Araiya," Jada said, smiling and hugging the older girl. "I do feel much better."

"You're welcome. You're going to do an amazing job as the Arctic Hare. Flopsy might want to hop on stage with you like Diggers," said Araiya, and the girls laughed even louder.

Chapter Seven
Relief

"See you at home Sky. Good luck with the lizards Nia. I'm pretty sure you have to be kissed by one before you turn into a lizard," Zane called as his mom pulled up.

"Not funny Zane!" called Nia, standing with her hands in her coat pockets and lips twisted into a smirk.

Dr. Washington's Fuzzy Friends Veterinary clinic was a quick walk down the tree-lined sidewalk. The girls could see their breath on each exhale. The chilly winter and need to be on time for their appointment pushed them to move quickly.

"I really don't want to do this," said Nia, rubbing the back of her ears peeking under the earmuff.

"If you want to dance as the

Lizard King, then the Snowbird says this is what we have to do," said Sky.

"Okay, already. Let's get this done, but you're one bossy Snowbird" said Nia.

"Bossy birds take care of business," said Sky.

"Is anyone else's nose frozen? It's not snowing, but that wind is whistling and I don't want to get a cold before the recital starts" said Jada, pulling her wool hat lower on her head. "Oh and sorry about Mr. Greedo, Nia. My brother wouldn't let me bring the gecko. He says it's too cold for Mr.

Greedo. I told him it was for a good cause, but he said Mr. Greedo wouldn't eat for weeks if we brought him out in this cold weather."

"That's ok, I wasn't looking forward to walking next to Mr. Greedo

anyway," said Nia.

The group stopped in front of two all glass doors. They could see an image of a cat chasing a dog and a bird standing on the side as the referee. The bird was so cute. He was wearing a black and white striped jersey and was blowing a whistle. The girls walked into the lobby and were greeted by Dr. Washington's receptionist. "Hi Mrs. Connie, is Dr. Washington still available to see us?" Sky asked.

"Yes of course. Sit right there and I'll let him know you're here. He's finishing up with his last patient. By the way, I already got my tickets for the recital. We can't wait to see the performance."

The vet clinic was definitely warmer than outside. The girls placed their scarves, hats and jackets on an empty seat. They sat on the cushy red chairs that surrounded a coffee table made from a long slab of wood. The large flat table looked like a tree split in half by a bolt of lightning. The girls looked around the room and Jada and Sky giggled at the framed pet *caricatures*. Nia sat statue-still waiting for the inevitable.

"Good afternoon Sky, Jada and Nia. I'm happy to get visitors at the

clinic. Especially young folks inter-
ested in veterinary science," said Dr.
Washington, entering from a pair of
swinging doors.

A green and brown lizard was balanced on top of his forearm like a loaf
of bread. The lizard looked at home
perched on the doctor's arm. There was
no flickering of the tongue, just the
tiniest of movements of the head as it
looked around the foyer. It didn't look
like it was trying to hypnotize anyone.
The doctor stopped at the receptionist
counter and handed Mrs. Connie the
lizard. She placed it inside of a large
aquarium with a heat lamp attached to

the top.

Dr. Washington kneeled down where the girls were sitting. "Congratulations on the upcoming Snowbird Ballet. My wife and I and all of the business owners in the plaza are coming to see you guys dance," said Dr. Washington.

"Thank you. We're excited and a little nervous about some of our parts," said Nia.

"Ah yes. Nia, Sky and Jada tell me you'd like to get to know more about reptiles; specifically, lizards. Have you had a chance to look through this book, *I'm Not Such a Terrible Lizard*?"

asked Dr. Washington.

"No sir, we hadn't noticed it. You have so many cool things to look at in here," said Sky.

"Well let's take a gander at a few pictures and you tell me what you think. Did you get my vet humor... gander, as in a male goose" said Dr. Washington as he began turning the pages. "Tell me, what do you think about dinosaurs?"

"I think dinosaurs are mega-cool. You get it Dr. Washington? Mega because they're big. And cool, because they're cold-blooded," said Nia, smiling at her own cleverness.

"Hehe, I'll have to remember that one," chuckled Dr. Washington.

"Do you young ladies know what the word dinosaur means?" he asked.

The girls shook their heads no.

"If we break the word apart, dino means fearfully great or terrible and saur means lizard... terrible lizard. Our modern day lizards are *descendants* of dinosaurs. Like dinosaurs, they're hatched from eggs and both have scales on their skin. They also have an endoskeleton."

"Oh that's the internal skeleton,"

said Nia when she saw her friends looking confused. "We talked about that at school."

"You got it. Take a look at these pictures and research on these two distant relatives. You might find they're quite beautiful. Nia, you can take this book home if you'd like," said Dr. Washington.

"I'd like that," Nia replied as she continued to look at the pictures of lizards and dinosaurs. "Oh, it says here that reptiles are beneficial to humans. Lizards eat lots of bugs humans don't like."

"Every species has a role to play in keeping our earth balanced. Most lizards are harmless to humans. A lot of them are like roaming pest control machines. Next time you see one, say thank you," said Dr. Washington.

"Would you guys like to meet Butter?" he asked, his knees creaking as he stood up. "Whew, I need you guys to go to vet school soon, these bones are getting older and ready to retire! I can see your compassion for each other and know you'll take good care of people and their pets."

The girls beamed as they crowded around the aquarium.

"Butter is a Bearded Dragon. She's staying with us a couple of weeks until her owners come back from Jamaica. Would you like to touch her?" asked Dr. Washington.

The girls took turns gently stroking Butter's back. Butter didn't move. She was falling asleep as the girls continued marveling over the smooth scales and spikey beard.

"We are totally gonna rock the Snowbird ballet," said Sky. The friends were smiling as Jada and Nia took a few steps away to do a *pirouette*.

"Nia, would you like to hold Butter?" asked Dr. Washington.

"I feel better about reptiles, Dr. Washington, but NOT that much better," said Nia, her head tilted to the side.

"Fair enough. I think our work is done here," said the doctor.

Chapter Eight
Bravo

"Dance strong, dance proud. Story
Bird Dance Academy!" the dancers
cried from their pre-performance
circle. They released hands and yelled,

"Break!"

"Let's get this!" said Ms. Kenya, squeezing the shoulders of several nearby dancers.

Sky took her place on the darkened stage. Her feather crowned head turned up, arms held in *second position*, she sat with her weight on one thigh, knees bent, toes pointed. The young Forget Me Not Fairies stood in a circle around her, holding a second position grand plie. Their blue and yellow tutus and black leotards mimicked the famous flower.

Jada, dressed as an Arctic Hare,

Nia, the Lizard King and Zane, a Polar Bear, stood off stage with the other dancers, waiting their turn.

A lighthearted drum beat sounded. The house lights rose and fell, alerting parents and friends to find their seats. The show was about to begin.

The heavy blue drapes parted in the middle, moving to the side to reveal a snow-dusted stage. The painted back-drop revealed ice-covered mountains with distant forget me not flowers blooming and thin cloud formations passing. The quiet steady drum loop quickened and grew deeper.

The Snowbird slowly rose as the Forget Me Not Fairies stood tall and began to *rolldown* curving their backs as they bent their heads forward, arms reaching down towards their toes and then rolling back up. The fairies grabbed each other's hands slowly raising and lowering them as the Snowbird continued to rise and stand tall.

Jada was focused and gracefully led the other Arctic Hares and Zane and all the Polar Bears across the snow-covered stage. The music and movement on stage entranced the entire audience. They watched as the hare, bear and fairies danced a good-bye and then a safe travel dance with their friend the Snowbird.

Everyone gasped as Nia, the Lizard King, leapt across the stage and brandished her long red claws and forced the Snowbird into an icy-

looking cage. The gold spotlight followed her and made the leotard scales sparkle. Nia twirled and slithered across the stage and danced the battle dance with the Arctic Hares and Polar Bears.

Parents and friends were on the edge of their seats when the Snowbird started spinning and freed herself from the icy cage. They were all clapping when the Lizard King met her end from one of the Snowbird's diamond eggs.

The performance was over and

the dancers ran on stage to take a bow.

Nia, Jada and Sky beamed at each other. They had faced their fears and won.

Playbill – The Snowbird
A Modern Ballet in Three Acts

Directed/Choreographed Ms. Kenya
Sky.................................Snowbird
Nia..............................Lizard King
Jada............................Arctic Hare
Zane............................Polar Bear
Little Dancers...........Forget Me Not Fairies
Little Dancers...........Leaf Lizards

80

ACT I
The Journey

Each winter the Snowbird flew from her Frozen Mountain home to cross the desert and lay her seven clear diamond eggs in the Valley of Hope. The Forget Me Not Fairies, Polar Bears and Arctic Hares danced around her to help her remember the way home once winter was over.

ACT II
Scene One - The Vision

The Lizard King ruled the area around the Valley of Hope. He granted the Snowbird passage through his land and into the valley. The Snowbird would give the Lizard King one of her eggs each year. He loved their shiny brilliance but, even more so, he loved that each egg allowed him to see into the future for one day. This ability allowed him to expand his kingdom. This year, when the Snowbird was ready to pass through the Lizard Kingdom he caught her and imprisoned her in a narrow icy cage. The Snowbird could only turn in circles and sing out from her prison.

ACT II
Scene Two - Lost

The Lizard King told her no one cared about her cries and that soon her friends would forget about the beautiful Snowbird. The Snowbird became sad and only laid two diamond eggs.

-Intermission-

ACT III

Freedom

As winter started to end the Snowbird's friends, the Polar Bears and Arctic Hares became worried. They went to search for her. An epic battle ensued. The Lizard King scratched one of the Polar Bears with his lethal claws. The Snowbird drew strength and size from watching her friends fight for her. She burst out of the cage and flew down into the battle with her two diamond eggs. She dropped one egg onto the head of Lizard King, knocking him out and she held her last egg over the injured Polar Bear. The Polar Bear's life was restored and the friends headed back to their frozen mountain home.

Wordlist

The Snowbird

Antagonist - a person who actively opposes someone or something

Catering - to supply food and drink at events

Chasse -a sliding dance step in which one foot chases the other. Like a gallop but with straighter legs. **Tour**-to turn. **Jete**- A jump in which a dancer leaps from one leg and lands on the other

Chasse Tour Jete - combining all three steps in order

Choreograph - to arrange or direct a sequence of movements

Cue - a signal to a performer to begin their performance

Empathize - to share the same feelings of another

First position - A posture in which the feet are turned outward with the heels touching

Pirouette - Whirl or spin. A complete turn of the body on one foot

Protagonist - the leading character or actor in a drama or real event

Second position - a posture in which the feet are turned outward with heels separated by a small step

45169959R00052

Made in the USA
Middletown, DE
26 June 2017